little owl,
keeper
of the trees

little owl, keeper of the trees

BY Ronald and ann himler

illustrations by Ronald himler

Harper & Row, Publishers
New York, Evanston, San Francisco, London

For Danny
For Anna

LITTLE OWL, KEEPER OF THE TREES
Text copyright © 1974 by Ronald and Ann Himler
Illustrations copyright © 1974 by Ronald Himler

LIBRARY OF CONGRESS CATALOG CARD NUMBER: 74-2615
TRADE STANDARD BOOK NUMBER: 06-022321-9
HARPERCREST STANDARD BOOK NUMBER: 06-022322-7

FIRST EDITION

contents

Little Owl
and
the Devil's Food Cake

Evening passed into darkness. The midsummer moon rose over the tops of the trees. It was night in the forest.

Little Owl climbed out of his bedroom window onto a limb of the old Sycamore Tree. Then he climbed up, first to one branch, then to another, and to another. There he sat.

He could see up and down the river. Moonlight shimmered on the water. He could see the deep green wood on the far shore, and in the distance the rising hills, where he had never been.

Little Owl turned around. He could see across the wild fields to the tall oaks at the edge of the gully. In the gully was a small stream that wound through the whole forest and flowed out into the big river.

He looked down. He could see the path at the bottom of the tree. His eyes followed the path down to the old bridge that crossed the stream.

Then he looked up, high up to the top of the Sycamore Tree. Someday, he thought, someday I'll climb all the way to the top. Then I'll sit up there in the night and hoot at the moon.

"Here sits Little Owl," he said to himself. "Guardian of the forest. Here sits the guardian of the forest, sharp-eyed, keen-eared, at the top of his mighty Sycamore Tree, watching over his kingdom."

"Little Owl!" Mrs. Owl called from below.

But Little Owl didn't hear her. "Here's the great night-watcher of the forest."

"Little Owl!" his mother called again. "Where are you?"

"Here's the great keeper of the trees. Here's the

guardian—Oh!" he slipped, "Oh!" and tumbled,
"Oh!" and fell down through the branches and
landed on the porch at his mother's feet.

"So there you are, Little Owl!" Mother said. "Are
you all right?"

"Of course," said the guardian of the forest, getting up.

"Listen to me, Little Owl," said Mother kindly. "How many times have I told you not to climb up the tree? You know you are afraid of high places."

"Yes, I know," said Little Owl. But someday, someday . . . he thought to himself.

"Breakfast is ready," said Mother.

Little Owl sat down to two big slices of toast with black-currant jam and a glass of milk. After breakfast he felt better. Mrs. Owl came out of the pantry carrying a basket.

"I want you to do something for me, Little Owl," she said. "Old Possum has a cold and isn't feeling very well. I made this devil's food cake to cheer him up. I want you to take it to him."

"Cake!" said Little Owl, peeking into the basket.

"Little Owl! Get your beak out of there!" His mother laughed. She covered the basket with a white cloth and gave it to Little Owl.

He took the basket and climbed down the steps of the old Sycamore Tree.

"Little Owl," Mother called from the porch. "Please don't daydream. Take good care of that cake."

Little Owl waved and walked down the path. A warm breeze rustled the trees. Little Owl could hear the frogs splashing down by the riverbank. Crickets chirped in the bushes.

Here's the guardian of the forest, thought Little Owl, bringing a gift of food to Old Possum.

As he went along the way, Little Owl stopped to watch the fireflies. They blinked all around him. Two fireflies landed on top of the basket.

"Hey, get off!" said Little Owl. "That is my mother's cake."

A family of field mice scurried across the path in front of him. Little Owl called out to them, but they were shy and quickly ran into the tall grass.

They must be new in the forest, thought Little Owl.

As he walked on, he began to feel tired. The basket was getting heavy. When he came to the old bridge, he decided to stop for a rest. He put the basket down and watched the water flow slowly underneath the bridge.

"Here's the guardian of the forest, resting on his long, hard journey." Little Owl yawned. Then he fell asleep.

When he woke up, the basket was empty.

"Hey, cake!" called Little Owl. "Where are you?"

Then he heard a noise. He stopped and listened. He listened very hard. It sounded like someone eating, and it came from under the bridge.

Little Owl leaned over the edge. .

"Hey!" he shouted. "Stop that! Whoever you are, stop eating my mother's cake!"

"My cake," said a deep voice.

"My cake," said Little Owl.

"My cake," said the voice again.

"Listen, you, under the bridge, you better come out of there and bring that cake with you!"

A small creature suddenly appeared on the railing of the bridge. Little Owl jumped back.

"My cake," said the creature in a friendly voice. And he took another bite.

"Who are you?" cried Little Owl.

"My name is Jonas," said the creature with a bow. He came dancing along the railing, nibbling on the cake, and suddenly vanished. He reappeared across the bridge and bowed again.

"I am Jonas, of the House of Benfras, of the Line of Bran. And the bridge is my home."

Then he looked at Little Owl. "And who are you?"

"I'm Little Owl. Little Owl of Sycamore Tree," said Little Owl nervously. "And you are eating my mother's cake!"

"And a very good cake it is," said Jonas.

He skipped three times to the left and began to sing. It was a strange, lilting song. It had no words except the sound of the wind. The melody seemed to cast a spell on Little Owl. He could not take his eyes off Jonas, who twirled and danced as he sang.

When the song was over, Jonas stopped right in front of Little Owl. His eyes were very bright. Little Owl shook his feathers, as though he were waking from a dream. When he looked again, Jonas was gone and so was the cake.

Little Owl was alone on the bridge. He did not know what to do. He began to cry.

"Certainly, owls don't cry over devil's food cake," said a deep voice.

Little Owl looked around. Jonas was standing in the empty basket.

"Why are you crying, Little Owl?" he asked.

"Because my mother baked that cake for Old Possum, who's sick. Now I have nothing to bring him and Mother will be angry."

"Ah," said Jonas. "I *am* sorry."

He came over and sat beside Little Owl. They sat together for a while and watched the water flow under the bridge.

Then Jonas spoke. "What's the matter with this Old Possum?"

"He has a cold," said Little Owl.

"Hmmm," said Jonas, thoughtfully. Then he got up, left the bridge, and wandered down among the bushes. He seemed to be looking for something. He bent down and spread the bushes gently with his fingers. Little Owl heard him talking to the plants.

"Come here, Little Owl," Jonas said. "I've found something that might help your friend."

Little Owl went over and stood beside Jonas.

"This is catnip," said Jonas.

"What nip?" asked Little Owl.

"Catnip," laughed Jonas. He pointed to a plant with gray-green leaves. There were clusters of small white flowers at the end of each branch. The edges of the leaves were ruffled.

"This is a mint," said Jonas. "It makes a very good tea. Just the thing for a cold."

Little Owl and Jonas filled the basket with catnip leaves. Then Jonas told Little Owl how to make the tea.

"Now, on your way!" he said.

Little Owl looked at Jonas.

"Don't worry," said Jonas. "Everything will be all right. You'll see."

Little Owl hurried off down the path toward Old Possum's house. He stopped for a moment and looked back at the bridge. He could not see Jonas, but he could hear the strange song once again.

"I'd better get going!" Little Owl said to himself.

There were lights on in Old Possum's house, but all the shades were pulled down. Little Owl rang the doorbell and waited for a long time. Old Possum came to the door, all bundled in blankets. His head was wrapped in hot towels.

"Good ebening, Little Owl," wheezed Old Possum. "Wad brigs you here?"

"I brought a present — from my mother," said Little Owl, nervously. "I hope you like it."

"Well, come in, Little Owl, and let's have a look."

Old Possum was very pleased with the present of catnip leaves. Together, they prepared the tea.

Then Old Possum invited Little Owl to stay for lunch. By the time they had finished, Old Possum was feeling much better. As Little Owl was getting ready to leave, Old Possum wrote a note and folded it.

"Give this to your mother," he said. "And thank you very much."

Little Owl walked back home through the forest. The moon was setting in the western sky. The crickets had stopped their singing, but here and there, a frog still croaked down by the riverbank.

When Little Owl got home, it was almost dawn. He gave the note to his mother, who was waiting for him.

It said:

Dear Mrs. Owl,

Thank you for the lovely present. It was just what I needed. I have already had two cupfuls and I feel much better.

Yours truly,
Old Possum.

Mrs. Owl looked puzzled.

"Old Possum certainly has a strange way of eating cake," she said. "By the cupful!"

Little Owl smiled.

Then he went out onto the porch. He stood looking down the path toward the bridge. Then he climbed out onto a big branch. He watched the great river flowing beneath the Sycamore Tree.

"Here sits the guardian of the forest, the keeper of the trees, the great helper and traveler, returned home."

little owl learns to fly

"Zoom!"

Little Owl jumped off the railing. He ran around the porch with his wings outstretched.

"Here's the great owl of the forest, sweeping over his kingdom. Zoom!" he cried.

He hopped back on the railing.

"Here's the great owl standing on the mountain-top. Now he takes to the air and flies away."

Little Owl jumped off the railing and ran around the porch again.

"Zoom. Z-z-z-z-z-z-zoom!"

He flapped his wings and ran around and around.

Then Little Owl stopped to rest. He climbed up the old Sycamore Tree and sat on a limb. Little Owl looked out over the great river. He saw a big riverbird swoop down into the water and come up with a fish in his beak. I wish I could fly like that, Little Owl thought.

The warm evening air was full of insects. Little Owl watched moths and fireflies hovering over the riverbank. A tiny mosquito came and buzzed in his ear. Little Owl listened.

How fast her wings must beat to make that sound, he thought.

Suddenly, a small brown bat darted out of the trees. He flew right past Little Owl and out over the river. Little Owl watched as he disappeared among the shadows on the far shore.

How quick Brown Bat flies, he thought.

Then he looked up. High overhead, way up in the darkening sky, a hawk circled. Hawk's great wings were outstretched, barely moving. Little Owl watched him for a long time.

How strong his wings must be, he thought. If I could fly like that, I'd soar to the top of the Sycamore Tree and hoot at the moon.

Little Owl heard splashing in the river. There were some ducks, getting ready to fly. It seemed to Little Owl that they ran across the water, flapping their wings. Then they rose into the air and flew away.

"Hey, that's what I need!" cried Little Owl. "A good running start." And he knew just the place.

"Zoom!" Little Owl climbed down the tree and ran down the path. He didn't stop running until he reached the top of a hill. He looked down the slope to an old log and a glade of soft grass beyond it. Little Owl took a deep breath and spread his wings. He ran down the hill as fast as he could. "Zoom!"

When he reached the log, he sprang into the air. He flapped his wings furiously. Little Owl saw his shadow in the moonlight on the grass below.

"Hey, I'm up! I'm up!" he cried. He hung in the air for a moment.

Then he was down.

Little Owl tumbled over in the soft grass. He placed a clump of red berries on the spot where he had landed. Then he counted the steps back to the old log to measure how far he had gone.

"Ten foot-lengths!" he cried. "I flew ten foot-lengths!"

He walked back up the hill.

Little Owl stood at the top and spread his wings. He raced down the hill in the moonlight. He beat his wings.

Suddenly, Little Owl began to rise into the air. He beat his wings harder. They lifted him higher. The forest and the glade whirled before his eyes. It made him dizzy. His wings wobbled.

Little Owl looked up, just in time. An old tree stood right in his path. He was heading straight for a big, low branch.

"Uh-oh!"

His feathers flew in all directions. Little Owl stuck out his feet. He tried to land, but he was going too fast. His feet missed the branch and he toppled over it.

Little Owl caught hold of the branch with his wing tips, just as he was about to fall. He hung in the air like an apple on a tree.

"Whew! Flying sure is hard work," he said.

But this was no place to rest. His wings ached

and the branch was slippery. He couldn't pull himself up. And it was too far down to let go.

Little Owl didn't know what to do.

Suddenly, a gust of wind shook the trees. Out of
the night, Jonas appeared on the branch above him.
He looked down at the hanging owl. His eyes
twinkled.

"Little Owl of Sycamore Tree, what are you
doing?"

"Oh, Jonas!" cried Little Owl. "Help me!"

Jonas bowed politely. "At your service."

31

He pulled Little Owl up by the tail feathers and sat him on the branch.

Little Owl rubbed his wing tips. "I'm learning how to fly!" he said proudly.

Jonas threw back his head and gave a deep, merry laugh. "And how does it feel?"

"Achy," said Little Owl. "I feel achy all over."

Jonas began to sing.

It was a song about birds flying on the wind. Sometimes he sang in a loud, clear voice. Sometimes he sang slow and soft. Just like the different winds that blow. Then he asked Little Owl to sing with him. Little Owl hesitated. He didn't know the words.

"Try," said Jonas.

Little Owl began to hum. Before he knew it, Little Owl was singing along with Jonas.

By the time the song was over, Little Owl wanted to sing it again. He especially liked the part about birds flying over the forest. That was what he wanted to do.

Jonas laughed and they sang the song again. When the song was over, Little Owl felt strong and rested. His achiness was gone. He got up and climbed down the tree.

"Little Owl of Sycamore Tree, where are you going?" Jonas called after him.

"I'm going to try again," said Little Owl.

"Wait, Little Owl. I'll come too."

Jonas sprang into the air and turned three somersaults that whistled like the wind. He landed on the grass next to Little Owl.

Little Owl could hardly believe his eyes. "How did you do that?" he asked.

"I rode on the wind," Jonas replied. "All creatures that fly ride on the winds, just as they do in the song."

"Yes!" said Little Owl excitedly. "This evening at sunset, I watched a hawk circling high in the sky. He didn't move his wings and he didn't fall."

"He was riding on the wind," said Jonas.

Little Owl went on. "A brown bat flew past me in

the Sycamore Tree, so fast I could hardly see him."

"He, too, was riding on the wind," Jonas replied.

"And mosquitoes, birds, and insects!" cried Little Owl.

"Yes." Jonas nodded. "They all ride on the wind." He turned and looked right into Little Owl's eyes.

Learn to know the winds,
How and when they blow.
Where they come from,
Where they go.

Jonas put his fingers to his lips and whistled softly.

Little Owl felt a sudden gust of wind at his back.

"Where did it come from?" Jonas asked.

"From behind me," said Little Owl.

"Where did it go?" Jonas asked.

"I don't know," answered Little Owl.

Then Jonas gave a shrill whistle.

A strong wind came and blew Little Owl over backward into the soft grass.

"Where did it come from?" asked Jonas.

Little Owl sat up. "It came from there and it's going that way," he said.

"Good," said Jonas. "The winds are my friends. They can be your friends, too, Little Owl."

"But how?" asked Little Owl.

"Ask the winds to help you fly," said Jonas.

Little Owl looked up. "Wind, please help me fly!"

Suddenly, a breeze came down the hill. It swept over the glade and scattered the red berries.

"There is your answer, Little Owl," said Jonas.

He danced and the moon grew bright.

Little Owl started back up the hill.

The clearing seemed to glow in the moonlight. Everything was very still. Little Owl was a small dark shadow at the top of the hill.

At a sign from Jonas, Little Owl spread his wings.

"Now, Little Owl, fly!" Jonas shouted.

Jonas began spinning around, faster and faster, making a sound like the wild wind.

"Fly, Little Owl, fly!" Jonas called.

Little Owl began running down the hill. He felt

the wind rush up to meet him. It pulled at his
wings. They began to flap. Little Owl felt the wind
carry him up off the ground.

"Beat a rhythm with your wings, Little Owl,"
called Jonas.

Little Owl began to count. "One-two. One-two."

He felt the wind rush under his wings and over
his head. He tipped his wings and flew in a circle.

Little Owl looked down. The glade was full of
forest creatures.

"Hey, everybody, I'm flying! I'm really flying!" Little Owl cried to them.

"Keep your rhythm, Little Owl," warned Jonas. "One-two. One-two."

Little Owl flew around and around the big old tree.

Then Jonas cried, "Come down now, Little Owl. Make a circle and land."

Little Owl circled the tree again. He spread the tips of his wing feathers and glided toward the soft grass. He stuck out his feet and got ready to land.

Thump! Little Owl hit the ground and rolled over. Jonas came and pulled him up by the tail feathers.

"Oh, Jonas, I can fly! I can fly!" cried Little Owl.

"Yes," laughed Jonas. "Just like a bird. But you must remember to thank the wind."

Little Owl spread his wings and danced. "Oh, thank you, Wind," he said. "Now I can fly."

Jonas began to sing. His song had no words except the sounds of the wind. The trees above them rustled and a wind blew over the glade.

Little Owl felt the whole forest dancing around him. Even the big moon seemed to smile.

BIRthDAYS

Little Owl rolled over in his bed and tucked the covers up around him. He listened to the rainfall on the leaves outside. He liked the sound of rain. He liked it so much he fell asleep.

When he woke up, the rain had stopped. Moonlight came through the bedroom window.

Suddenly, Little Owl sat up.

"Tonight is my birthday!" he cried aloud. He threw back the covers and ran into the kitchen.

"Good evening, Little Owl." His mother smiled. "Are you ready for breakfast?"

"I'm hungry," said Little Owl, sitting down at the table. "Do you know what tonight is?"

"Yes, I do," said Mrs. Owl, as she put two big slices of toast with black-currant jam before him. "Tonight is the night I must clean the cupboards."

"No, no!" said Little Owl. "I mean, do you know what *tonight* is? It's special."

"There's nothing special about cleaning cupboards," said Mother, laughing. She poured Little Owl a glass of milk and went back to her work.

After breakfast, Little Owl went outside. "She forgot," he said to himself, going down the steps of the old Sycamore Tree. "She forgot that tonight is my birthday. This never happened before." Little Owl sighed.

A cool breeze was scattering the last of the rain clouds. Stars twinkled in the patches of clear sky.

Little Owl walked slowly out into the wild fields. The high, wet grass glistened like silver in the

moonlight. Little Owl brushed back the wet grass with his wing and the grass sprang back, showering him with raindrops. It tickled, and this made him laugh.

As he came to the tall oaks at the edge of the field, he saw Raccoon sitting beneath a tree.

"Hi, Raccoon," said Little Owl. "Do you know what tonight is?"

"You bet I do," said Raccoon.

"You do?" cried Little Owl.

"Tonight's the night my cousin promised to show me his secret fishing place."

"Oh," said Little Owl. "I thought you *knew*."

"I've been waiting here since sunset," Raccoon went on, "but he hasn't come yet. Well, I can't wait any longer. I'm going down to the old rock by the river and fish."

"Can I come?" asked Little Owl.

"Listen, Little Owl," said Raccoon. "You know what you can do? When my cousin comes by, tell him I'm down at the river. Will you do that, Little Owl?"

Then Raccoon hurried off without waiting for an answer.

Little Owl was left alone in the moonlight. He stood for a while, looking down the path. But no one came.

I'm not going to stand here all night, he thought. Not on my birthday.

Little Owl wrote a note for Raccoon's cousin and stuck it on the tree. Then he stepped back and looked at the note.

Suppose, he thought, suppose that note was a sign that said, "Tonight is Little Owl's birthday." And there were signs just like it all over the forest. Then everyone would know about my birthday.

"Everyone!" he cried aloud. "That's it—I'll make signs."

Little Owl ran back through the wild fields, with his wings out, making the raindrops fly. He laughed all the way across the fields.

He went into the cellar of the old Sycamore Tree. There, among all the dusty chests, boxes, picture frames, and cans of paint, he found a stack of boards.

Little Owl spread all the boards out in the middle of the floor. Then he opened a can of blue paint. He dipped the tip of one feather into the paint and wrote on the first board: "Tonight is Little Owl's birthday."

I'll put this sign down by the river, Little Owl thought. He painted some water at the bottom of the sign to remember where it should go.

Then he dipped another feather into a can of green paint. "I'll put this sign on the old tree in the hollow," he said. So he painted some leaves at the bottom of the sign.

Next, Little Owl dipped another feather into the red paint. "I'll put this one on the bridge," he said. And he carefully drew a picture of the old bridge at the bottom of the sign.

He dipped another feather into the yellow paint. "I'll put this one by the wild fields." Little Owl painted tall grass all around the edge of the sign.

Then he started all over again, first with the blue, then the green, then the red, and last the yellow. He went on in this way until all the boards were painted. On each sign he painted a mark, so he would remember where to put it.

When he was done, Little Owl looked at his wing. Each feather was a different color. He liked it so much, he dipped his other wing in the colors, too.

"Now I even look like a birthday owl." He laughed.

Little Owl picked up all the signs and carried them off down the path.

"Here's the guardian of the forest, the keeper of the trees, bringing an important message to all the creatures in the forest," Little Owl said to himself.

51

The path led away from the river into the deep woods. At the edge of the hollow was a great maple tree that had been split by lightning. Into the crack of the tree, Little Owl wedged the green sign.

He stepped back to see how it looked. It fell down.

"Phooey!" said Little Owl. He picked up the sign and wedged it in again.

Again it fell out.

"I'll just have to go back and get a hammer and nail it up," said Little Owl.

He left the pile of signs near the bottom of the tree and went home.

When he came back, all the signs were gone. Someone was hammering furiously down in the hollow. Little Owl left the path and went down into the low hollow.

It was a damp, lonely place, overgrown with clumps of sedge grass and brambles. The trees were old, and their roots twisted and stuck out above the ground. The cool night breeze had scattered the mists which usually hung over the hollow.

Suddenly, the hammering stopped. Mole poked his head around the stump of a tree.

"Is that you, Little Owl?" he said in a slow, sad voice. "It's me—Mole."

"Hello, Mole," said Little Owl. "I haven't seen you in a long time."

"No one usually does," said Mole. He came around and sat on a gnarled root in front of Little Owl. "But I saw you, Little Owl," he said shyly. "Yes I did."

Mole sat with his head down, staring at his toes. "Oh, Little Owl, you have made me very happy," he said.

"I have?" asked Little Owl. "You don't look happy."

"Oh, I always look like this," sighed Mole. "But tonight, I *am* happy. Do you know what tonight is, Little Owl?"

"I do!" said Little Owl excitedly. "Do you know?"

"Tonight is my birthday," said Mole, proudly.

"*Your* birthday!" gasped Little Owl.

"Every year tonight is my birthday," Mole went on, "but no one ever knows. I don't suppose it really matters much, though it does make a difference somehow. But you remembered, Little Owl."

"I did?" asked Little Owl.

"Yes, you did," Mole continued. "You said to yourself, 'Tonight must be Mole's birthday and I'm going to make him a wonderful present.' So you made that present, Little Owl. You brought it here and set it down near my hole. Then you hurried off so that I would be surprised.

"But I saw you, Little Owl. I was just poking around here, all by myself, as usual, when I saw you do it.

"Oh, Little Owl," said Mole, getting up slowly, "I'm so happy! Come and see."

Mole led Little Owl down to a corner of the hollow. "Look!" he said proudly.

"My signs!" cried Little Owl.

"My new house," sighed Mole. "Isn't it beautiful?"

Little Owl could hardly believe his eyes. Mole was building a house out of Little Owl's signs.

"I've always wanted a real house," said Mole. "And now, because of your wonderful present, I shall have one. I'll sit in it all day long and look at the lovely decorations you painted for me."

Mole could not read. In fact, he could not even see very well.

"Oh, it will be a happy home," said Mole. "And a happy birthday."

Little Owl looked at his signs. Some of them were already nailed together. "Now no one will ever know," he sighed to himself.

Then Little Owl looked at Mole's happy face. He picked up his hammer and helped Mole build his house.

He nailed the blue board to the red, red to the yellow, green toward the door. That's the way Mole liked it.

When they were finished, they sat together on a small stump and admired the house.

"Do you know what tonight is, Mole? Tonight is my birthday, too," said Little Owl, beaming.

"Your birthday and my birthday on the same night?" cried Mole.

"That's right," said Little Owl. "Let's go to my house and celebrate our birthdays together."

Mole was delighted. He had never celebrated anything with anyone before.

Little Owl and Mole came out of the hollow and together they started down the path. The deep night sky was filled with stars. Fireflies blinked at them from the shadows of the wood. Crickets sang under the leaves. On the way home, Little Owl taught Mole a birthday song.

They climbed the steps of the old Sycamore Tree. A glow of colored lights came from the kitchen window.

Little Owl opened the door.

"Surprise!" everyone shouted. "Happy birthday, Little Owl!"

Little Owl couldn't believe his eyes. The kitchen was all decorated with lights and colored paper. The table was set for a party.

Around it stood Raccoon and his cousin, Old Possum and his nephew, the gray rabbit and his sister, and all Little Owl's friends.

Mole was so startled, he hid behind Little Owl. "What's going on?" he asked timidly.

"It's a birthday party!" cried Little Owl.

He ran over to his mother and gave her a big hug. "You remembered after all!"

"Remembered what?" His mother laughed.

"You remembered my birthday. And it's Mole's birthday, too," said Little Owl.

Mole was still standing back in the doorway. Little Owl brought him right into the middle of the party.

"Happy birthday, Mole," said Mrs. Owl.

"Happy birthday, Mole. Happy birthday, Little Owl!" everyone cried in one voice.

I wonder if Jonas knows it's my birthday? Little Owl thought. I wonder if he'll come?

Just then, Mrs. Owl said, "Little Owl, you left the door open."

"No," said Little Owl. "I closed it when we came in."

As Little Owl went over to close the door, he looked around the room. "I wonder . . ." he said to himself.

Then Mrs. Owl brought out a big cake with HAPPY BIRTHDAY spelled out in black currants. Little Owl set an extra place beside himself and, when the cake was served, he put one piece in front of the empty place.

"Who is that for?" asked Mrs. Owl.

"Oh," said Little Owl. "That's just in case someone should drop by."

Everyone ate and laughed together. Then they all sang songs. Mole sang the birthday song Little Owl had taught him.

When the singing stopped, a clear deep melody of a strange song seemed to linger in the air. Then it faded, like the wind.

"Who was that singing?"

Everyone looked at everyone else, except Little Owl, who looked at the empty place.

The piece of cake was gone.

His eyes brightened. Little Owl quietly lifted the tablecloth and peeked under the table.

There sat Jonas, with an empty plate on his knee.

"Your cake," Jonas whispered. "And a very good cake it is.

"Happy birthday, Little Owl."